A VERY MOO-EY

Christmas

Mark Bradley

MARK BRADLEY

PAGE PUBLISHING, INC.
Conneaut Lake, PA

First originally published by Page Publishing 2021

ISBN 978-1-6624-2865-4 (hc)
ISBN 978-1-6624-2864-7 (digital)

Printed in the United States of America

To my little farmers Parker and Alexa. Always
follow your dreams, and never give up.

To my wife and best friend Nichole. Thank you for always
supporting and encouraging me in everything I do.

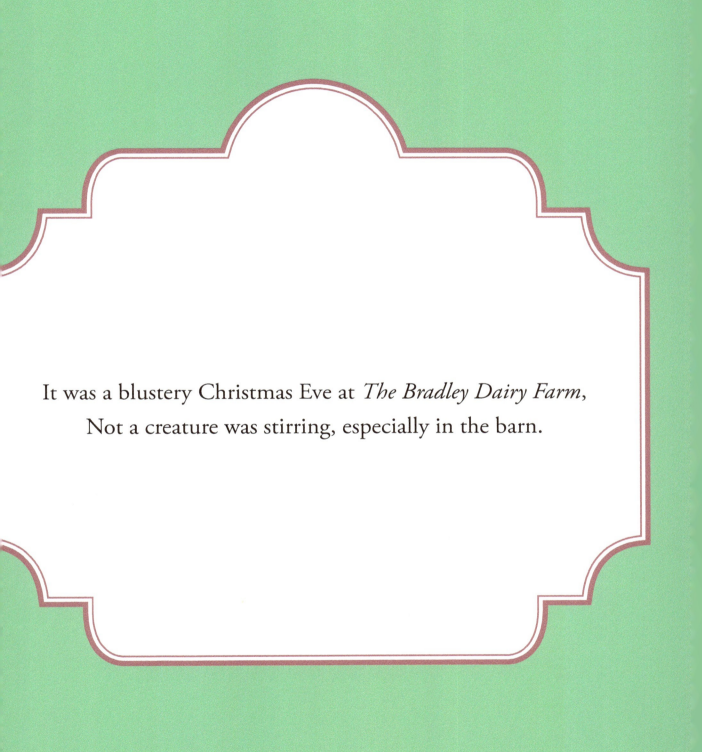

It was a blustery Christmas Eve at *The Bradley Dairy Farm*,
Not a creature was stirring, especially in the barn.

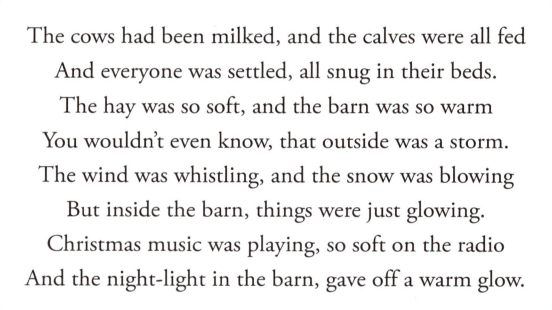

The cows had been milked, and the calves were all fed
And everyone was settled, all snug in their beds.
The hay was so soft, and the barn was so warm
You wouldn't even know, that outside was a storm.
The wind was whistling, and the snow was blowing
But inside the barn, things were just glowing.
Christmas music was playing, so soft on the radio
And the night-light in the barn, gave off a warm glow.

4

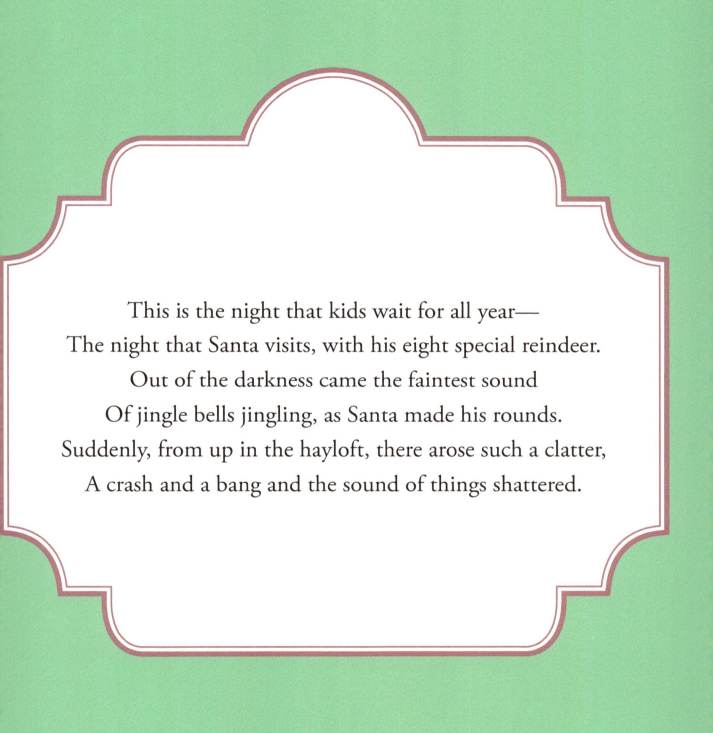

This is the night that kids wait for all year—
The night that Santa visits, with his eight special reindeer.
Out of the darkness came the faintest sound
Of jingle bells jingling, as Santa made his rounds.
Suddenly, from up in the hayloft, there arose such a clatter,
A crash and a bang and the sound of things shattered.

Holly awoke from a deep, peaceful sleep,

She jumped out of her stall and sprang straight to her feet.

"What was that noise?" her voice quivered with fear.

"It's okay," her mom replied, "Santa must be here."

Then as if out of nowhere, there appeared such a sight,

The jolly man himself, was standing under the night-light.

9

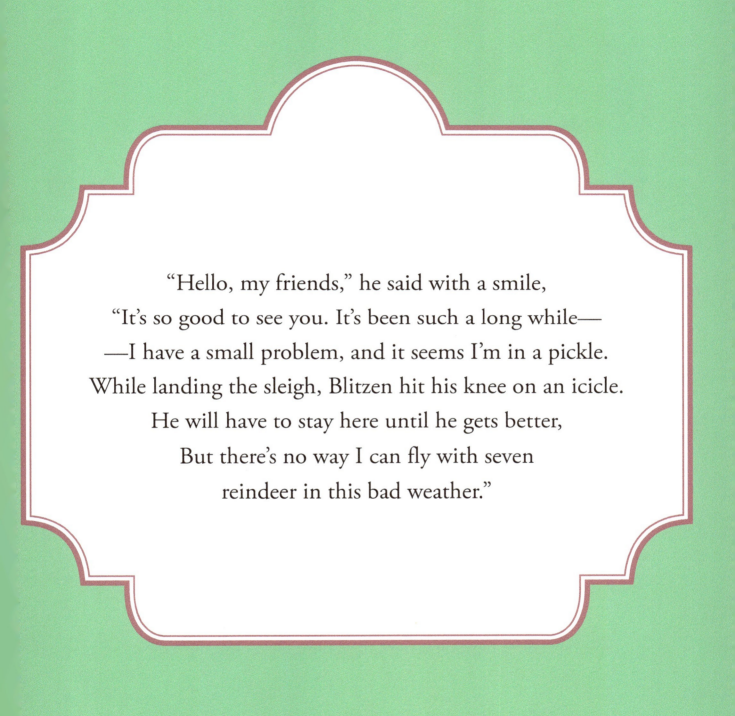

"Hello, my friends," he said with a smile,
"It's so good to see you. It's been such a long while—
—I have a small problem, and it seems I'm in a pickle.
While landing the sleigh, Blitzen hit his knee on an icicle.
He will have to stay here until he gets better,
But there's no way I can fly with seven
reindeer in this bad weather."

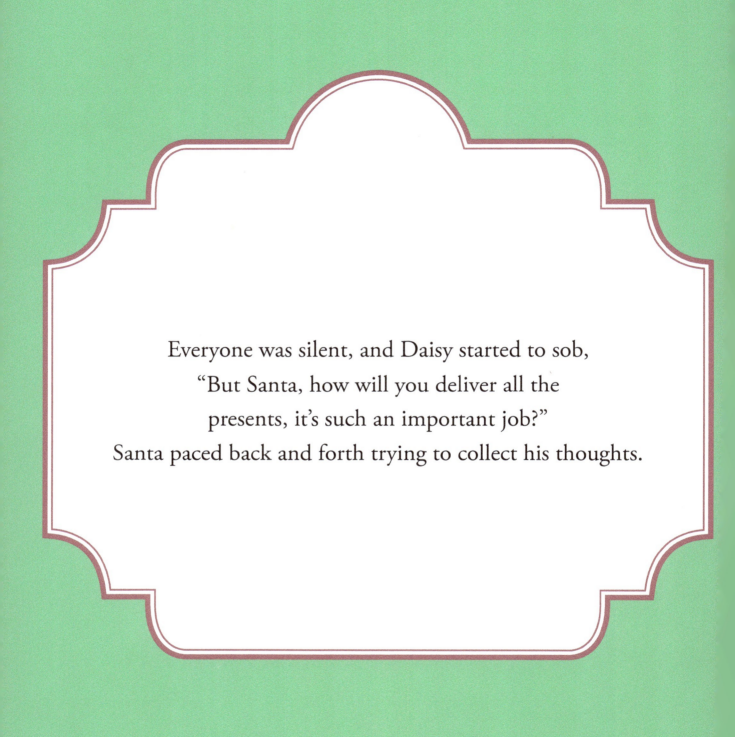

Everyone was silent, and Daisy started to sob,
"But Santa, how will you deliver all the
presents, it's such an important job?"
Santa paced back and forth trying to collect his thoughts.

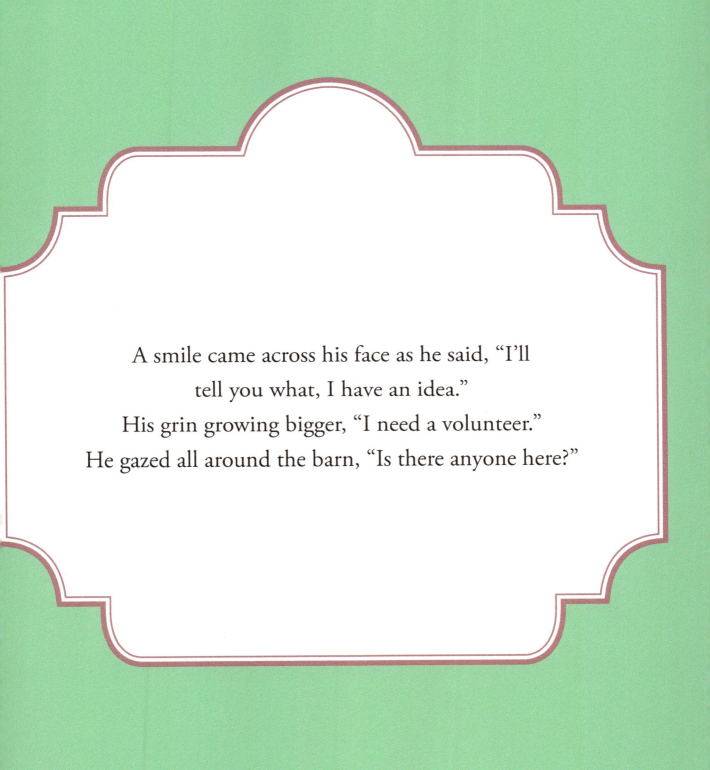

A smile came across his face as he said, "I'll
tell you what, I have an idea."
His grin growing bigger, "I need a volunteer."
He gazed all around the barn, "Is there anyone here?"

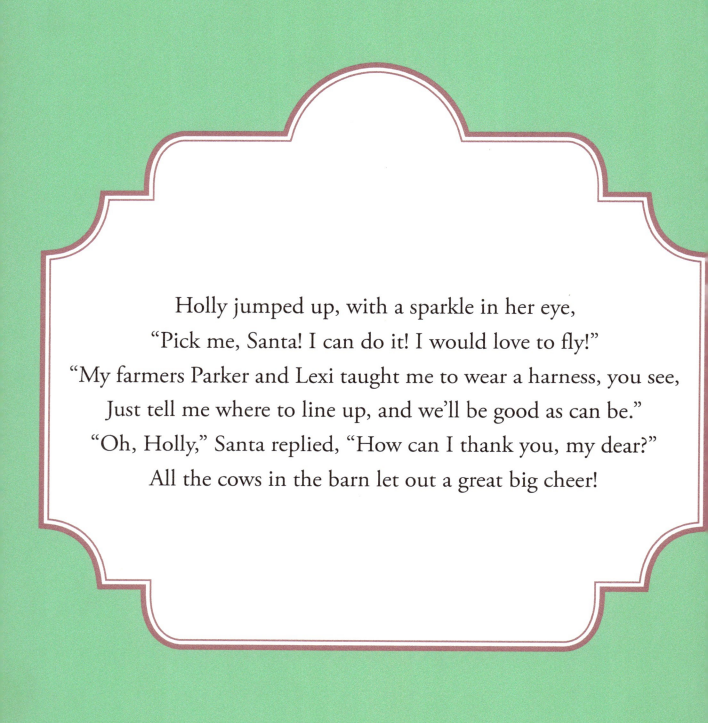

Holly jumped up, with a sparkle in her eye,

"Pick me, Santa! I can do it! I would love to fly!"

"My farmers Parker and Lexi taught me to wear a harness, you see,

Just tell me where to line up, and we'll be good as can be."

"Oh, Holly," Santa replied, "How can I thank you, my dear?"

All the cows in the barn let out a great big cheer!

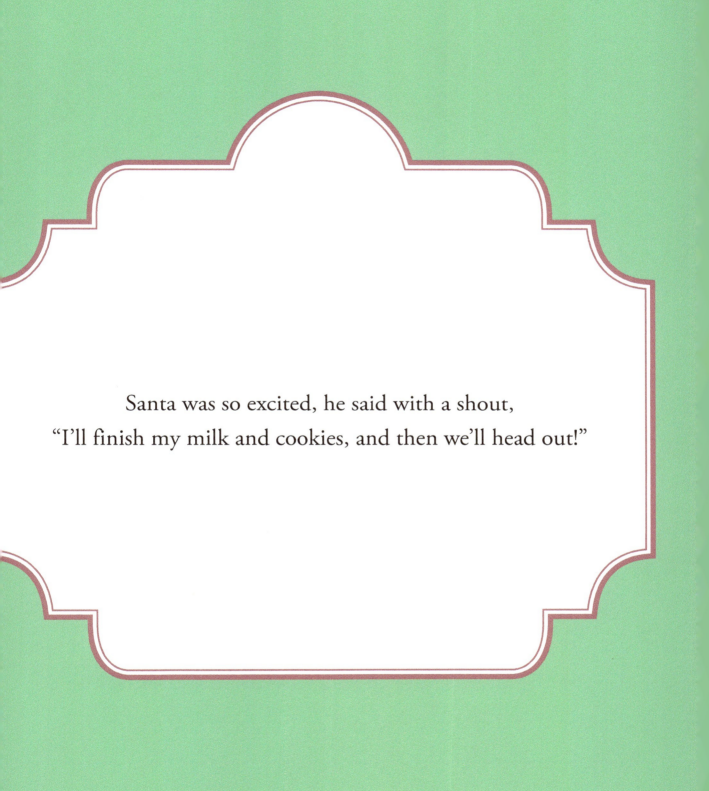

Santa was so excited, he said with a shout,
"I'll finish my milk and cookies, and then we'll head out!"

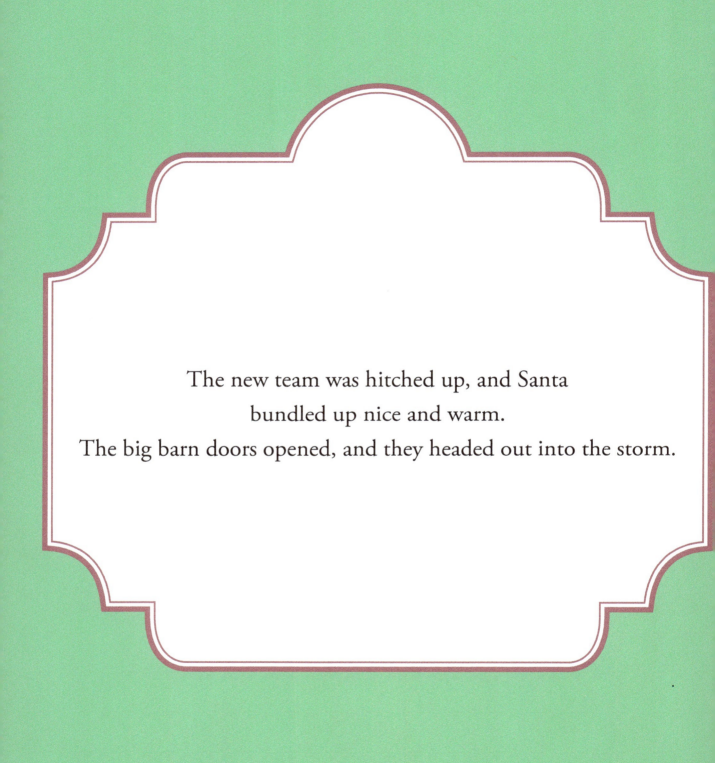

The new team was hitched up, and Santa
bundled up nice and warm.
The big barn doors opened, and they headed out into the storm.

21

From his perch upon his sleigh, he called out to his team.
Holly was so excited, now she was living her dream.
"On Dasher, on Dancer, on Prancer, and Vixen,
On Comet, on Cupid, on Donner, and Holly!"
All together the team pulled, and the big sleigh took flight.
The storm was fierce, but they pulled with all their might.

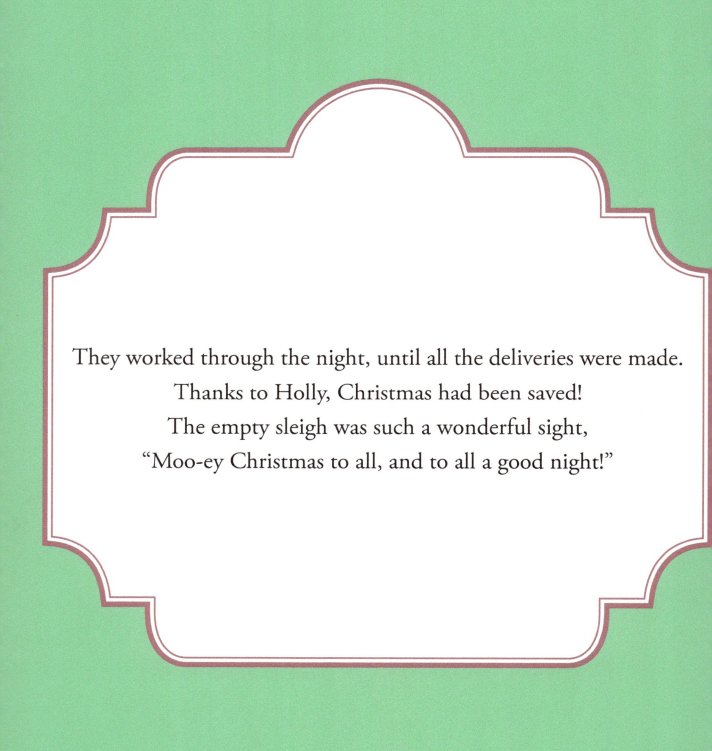

They worked through the night, until all the deliveries were made.

Thanks to Holly, Christmas had been saved!

The empty sleigh was such a wonderful sight,

"Moo-ey Christmas to all, and to all a good night!"

24

About the Author

Mark Bradley is a second-generation dairy farmer from Athens, Pennsylvania. He operates a fifty-cow dairy in partnership with his father on the farm where he grew up. Mark started an Adopt a Calf program in 2018, where he shares his passion about dairy farming in local schools and within the community. This hands-on program inspired him to write *A Very Moo-ey Christmas*. He lives with his wife, Nichole, children Parker and Alexa, and their many pets.

CPSIA information can be obtained
at www.ICGtesting.com
Printed in the USA
BVHW062242290821
615191BV00001B/4